First Grade, Here I Come!

To Desmond —T. J.
Especially for my friend Grayson —D. W.

Text copyright © 2015 by Roger D. Johnston and Susan T. Johnston,
as Trustees of the Johnston Family Trust.
Illustrations copyright © 2015 by David Walker

ISBN 978-0-545-20144-5

12 11 10 9 8 7 6 5   17 18 19 20 21

Printed in the U.S.A.   08
First printing 2015
Book design by Chelsea C. Donaldson

First Grade, Here I Come!

by
Tony Johnston

pictures by
David Walker

Scholastic Inc.

I'm zooming off to first grade now.
I need about five friends
to play good games like hide-and-sneak
and where-the-sidewalk-ends.

Then all of us will crouch around
like tigers on the prowl.
We'll lash our tails and flash our eyes
and clash our fangs and growl.

My teacher will be thrilled to bits
'cause we can count—wahoo!—
a million and a trillion
and a skilly-skillion too.

We'll all be veggiesaurs that eat
our veggies quick-quick-quicks.
At snacktime we'll all chomple down
carrots and celery sticks.

We'll help the teacher decorate
and sing a swoopy song.
Our paper chains will swag the room.
(We're big, so they'll be long.)

My friends and I will make a band
that *rum-tum-tummy-tums*.
We'll boom around the room and beat
on oatmeal-carton drums.

The bunch of us will read, oh read.
We'll know a lot of words—
rhinoceros, preposterous,
and cassowary birds.

In winter we will all be bears.
(Bears don't wear shirts or sleeves.)
We'll snort up from our winter sleeps
and romp in piles of leaves.

I'll need at least five friends to play
the *Rubber Family.*
We'll stretch our faces and ourselves
like pretzels. Tee-hee-hee!

A B C D E F G

For show-and-tell, no teddy bears.
I'll bring my snake — oh, joy!
My friends will hold my boa up.
(I call him Huggy Boy.)

We'll all be space guys in fat suits,
so bold and brave and big.
Our mascot will be brave and pink.
Oh, he will be a pig.

At recess we'll be super guys.
We'll all screech "Zippy-do!"
And dash around all full of zoom.
We'll all be Captain True.

We'll climb the jungle gym for sure
and dangle by our knees;
We'll chitter-chatter all the time
like chatty chimpanzees.

If one of us scrapes up a knee
and bleeds a little bleed,
of course, we'll all go to the nurse.
His friends are what he'll need.

We'll do a neat-o dragon play.
We'll be the guys who yelp
when dragons come to scorch them up.
Our lines are: *"Help! Help! Help!"*

It's plain to see I need five friends.
Yep, five would be fine fun.

But no, I think I'd rather be
good friends with—EVERYONE!

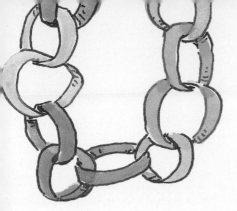
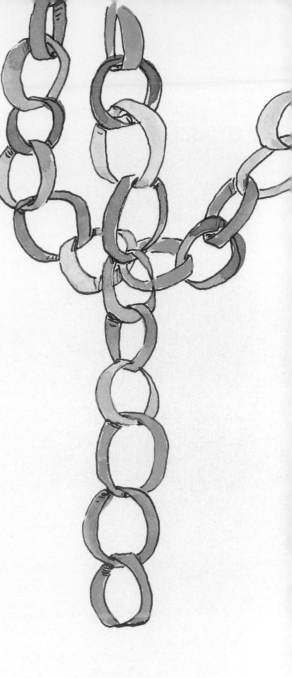